Abdallah
ABDULKARIM
Abdulrahman
Abla
ABRIL
Adam
Ahmed
Ai
AILBHE
Aina
Aisling
Aitor
Alaa
ALEJANDRA
Alessio
ALEXAI
Ali
ALMA
Alperen
Alvaro
Amal
Amani
AMARI
Amber
ANAS
Aniessa
Annette
Antonija
Aodhen
Aoibhinn

Aoiffe
Aotao
Arda
Ariadna
ARMEN
Arnav
Arwa
Aseal
Asem
Assma
Ava
Awad
Badr
BAO
Bassem
Batuhan
BAUTISTA
Beatriz
Bedirhan
Beyza
Biel
BILAL
BIYU
Boadicea
BOGDAN
Bohua
Bronimir
Buglem
Bunyamin
Burak

Callum
Caoimhe
Cesar
Chaker
CHANGMING
Cheng-En
CHEYANNE
Clodagh
Concepcion
Dana
Dahlia
Danene
Duarte
Darragh
DINI
Dunia
Ebubekir
Efe
Eleni
Elissa
Emiliano
EMIRHAN
Eoghan
Erdem
Esma
Fabian
Fatima
Fawzieh
Fei

Felipe
FIADH
Firas
Franjo
Geonwoo
GABRIEL
GINEVRA
Giovanni
Giulia
Giuseppe
GUANG
Guilherme
GULPARI
Guoliang
Habeeba
Hadi
Haeun
Haider
HAIZEA
Hamza
Hanya
Harun
Hatem
Hatice
Hazem
HIKMAT
Hind
HIRANUR
Hoa
Hodaya
HUANG

Huizhong

Khaled

Maja

MIROSLAVA

Ibuki

HyAlood

Malalai

Mirvat

Ichika

Khelwa

Malek

Muhammed

Ido

Kokona

Malik

MOHANAD

Imak

Ksenia

Mansi

Moina

Irati

Kuzey

Mao

MOMOKA

ISADORA

Lachlan

Marcello

Mousa

Issa

LAI

MARIAM

Mustfa

Itamar

Lamis

Mariana

Nadezhda

Izan

Lara

Maryam

Nadira

Jacopo

Layla

Mathis

NAJLA

Jaime

Leah

Matias

Najeeb

JALIA

Lei

Matteo

Namah

Naomi

For my amazing mother,
whose unconditional love and excellent guidance
has been my life's most priceless gift.

Javed

Lena

Matvei

Nassrine

Javier

LI

Medina

Neda

Jayesh

Lieke

Mehmet

Nehir

JELENA

Lihua

Meihui

Nehorai

Jenna

Lilou

Mert

NGUYEN

JIAO

LINH

Melehan

Nhung

Jimena

Ljubina

Miereia

Niamh

JIWOO

LOORA

Milan

Noemi

Joao

Lorcan

MILO

NOOR

Joonsun

LUCIA

Minal

Nouralhouda

Juan

Lotte

Minh

Oceanne

Carlos

Ludovica

Minjae

OIER

Juana

LUUK

Mirac

Olson

Kaidhum

Maha

Onab

Khadija

Maite

~~Tell~~ *Teach* Us Your Name

By Huda Essa
(hood-deh ee-sseh)
Illustrated by Diana Cojocaru
(dye-anna co-jo-carroo)

It was the first day of school and the words I dreaded hearing tumbled out of my teacher's mouth.

In a cheerful voice, she said, "Now, I'm going to take attendance. Please raise your hand when you hear your name. Oh, and please correct me if I'm saying it wrong."

She sent all the students warm smiles after reading their names.
"Paul? ...Kathy? ...Melanie?"

I cringed, knowing my name would come soon.
"...David? ...Paula?"

Then, it happened...

I saw her smile fade, her eyes squint
and her lips purse together like she
was trying to figure out a tricky puzzle.

She quietly cleared her throat. "Well,
let me see if I can get this one... Is it
Karma-lie-yee-zeen-aid-een? Am I saying
it right?" Her voice swelled with hope.

I bashfully nodded my head.

"Okay, good." She smiled with relief
and content.

I was too embarrassed to look up again, afraid I'd see others laughing at me. My teacher continued with attendance, but the only voice I could hear was the one in my head...

My name is pronounced Kareema-lay-yes-seen-a-deen. Ugh! I haaaaate my naaaame! Why do I have to have the **ugly**, TERRIBLE, WEIRD and ridiculously long name?

As soon as we got home, my brother quickly started speaking. "Mama, Kareemalayaseenadeen said she hates her name. She even said she's mad at you and Baba for naming her something so ugly."

"I can't believe you!" I shouted at him, jumping up as he snickered and ran away.

"Is that true?" Mom sounded disappointed.

Through clenched teeth, I answered, "Yes. Why couldn't you have given me an easy name, like the ones the other kids at school have?"

"Oh? What names are those?" she asked calmly.

I stomped my foot. "Like Patricia or Jennifer or something."

She looked confused. "Those names are easy for *you* to say, but for *other* people they may be hard to say. The same is true of your name.

No one had ever actually told me that my name was **ugly**, TERRIBLE and WEIRD. But they didn't have to; I already knew it was.

When we learned about history in school, no famous person shared *my* name. I would often find my friends' names in books, but *my* name never appeared.

The characters in my favorite TV shows and movies? Yeah, they never had *my* name either.

Trying to squeeze my name into spaces made for normal names was becoming a pain.

I never found a bracelet, mug, or even a flimsy keychain with *my* name on it. My mom tried to buy me a special bracelet but was charged additional fees for all the extra letters! Then it was too long to be a bracelet anymore, so we had to change it into a necklace.

One of my classmates pointed out that my name was almost as long as the alphabet. When he said that to the *whole class*, he was smiling but I was not.

My teachers and classmates began calling me "Karma-deen." I was too shy to correct them. Eventually, even though I hated it, that's what I started calling myself, too. It was just easier that way.

Then in one wonderful summer, Mama and Baba took us on an overseas trip to visit family. We spoke a different language there and got to see new places and friendly faces. Every day felt like a new adventure!

My grandma, Sittee, was one of my favorite people there. Everyone loved listening to her stories, which always seemed to hold valuable lessons.

One afternoon, in a matter-of-fact voice, she said, "My dear, your mother tells me you are having troubles with your name."

It was only then that I realized I hadn't thought about my name once the entire trip. Everyone there seemed to have already heard of it, and most people had nice things to say about it.

Her voice was soft as she asked, "Do you know what your name means, Kareemalayaseenadeen?"

I thought about it for a moment and then shook my head.

With a tender smile, she said, "Your name is a beautiful word that means 'excellent guidance,' and it is a big part of who you are. If you hate your name, you are hating an important part of yourself."

"But where I live, it's so hard for people to say my name," I replied.

"Maybe so, but your name means 'guidance.' So why don't you guide them on the proper way to say your name?"

She leaned in and gave me a big kiss on the cheek.

I thought a lot about what Sittee said. On our
long flight returning home,
I brainstormed a plan
for how I could guide
others to correctly
say my name.

I stuck to my plan and kindly corrected anyone who mispronounced my name, *teaching* them how to pronounce it the way I wanted it to be said. I started to think that maybe I really was good at this guidance stuff, which made me want to do it even more... and that is exactly what I did.

Kareema - lay -

I became a teacher! And every year, on the first day of school, I asked my students to *teach* me their names. Guiding people to take pride in who they are was so important to me that I even wrote a book about it! You're reading it now...

And my *lovely*, meaningful, *unique* name is finally in a book that I want to read.

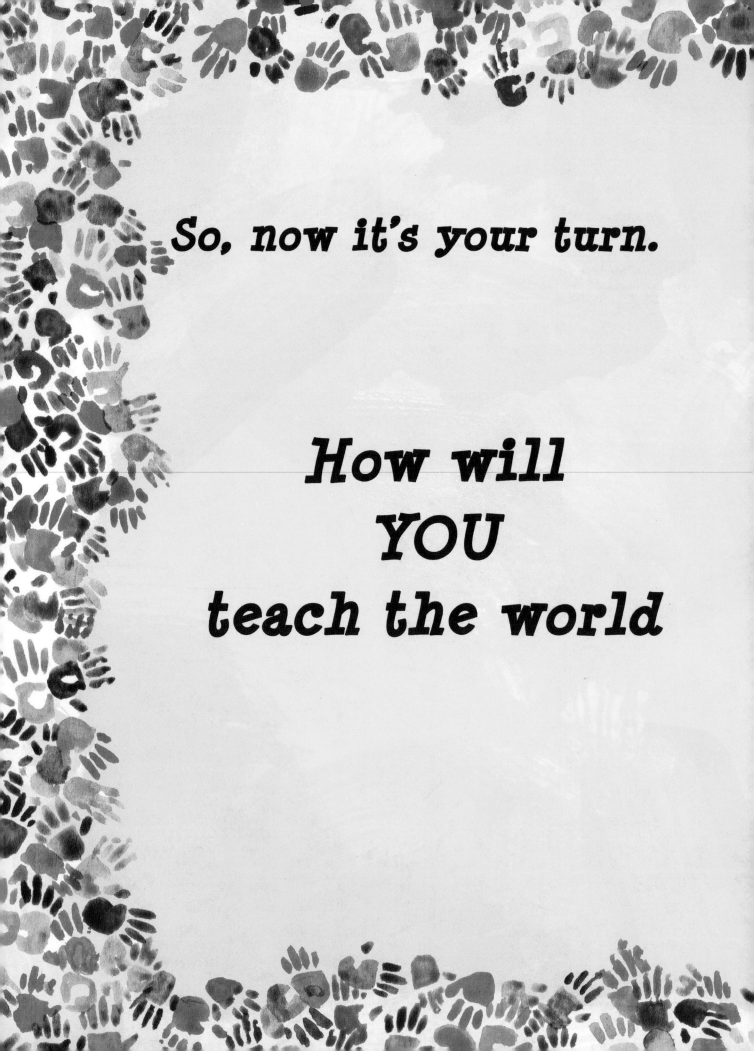

So, now it's your turn.

How will
YOU
teach the world

your

WONDErFUL

amazing

terrific

name?

Okot
Othman
Paola
Pau
Peizhi
Persephone
PETRONILLA
Phuong
Pietro
Pin-Jui
Po-Yu
Pratima
Praveen
QUAN
Quyen
Rada
Radimir
Radko
Raja
Randa
raneem

Reina
Reyam
Rima
Rivka
Ronya
Rose
Rosetta
Rula
Ryuga
Ryuto
Sadhbh
Sahil
Samaher
Santiago
Semyon
Seppe
SHIBAM
Shiori
soraya
Sroa
Stanislav
Suad

Sudenaz
Tahel
taisei
Tariq
THANH
Thiago
Thijs
timofe
Timur
Tommas
Tugba
TUUR
Umar
Unal
Utkarsh
Uxue
Vania
Varvara
Vasil
VEDrana
Vihaan
Vimena
VLADISLAV
Voeddog
Walleed
woojin
Xandra
Xenia
Xiang
Xiao-ping

Xing-fu
Xing
Xiu
Yagmur
Yanis
Yeeun
Yehia
Yekaterina
Yelyana
Yonata
Yoonsuh
Youssef
Yu-En
Yu-Hsiang
Yui
YUTA
Yuzukis
Zahia
Zainab
Zaid
Zehra
Zhanna
Zlata
Zvonimir

Now,
add your names!

ISBN-13: 978-0692695326 (Custom Universal)
ISBN-10: 069269532X

55816527R00020

Made in the USA
Charleston, SC
05 May 2016